Dear Baby,

Dedicated to my mom, Amy Krouse Rosenthal.
I will forever be your baby. —P.R.

Dear Christy,
My superhero agent and my sweet friend. Thank you for
changing the course of my life and making my childhood
dreams come true. This book is for you. xox
—H.H.

Special thanks to Luana Horry

Library of Congress Control Number: 2019956239
ISBN 978-0-06-301272-1

The artist created the illustrations digitally for this book.
20 21 22 23 24 PC 10 9 8 7 6 5 4 3 2 1
❖
First Edition

Dear Baby,

A love letter to little ones

by PARIS ROSENTHAL ★ illustrated by HOLLY HATAM

HARPER
An Imprint of HarperCollinsPublishers

Dear Baby,

Welcome to this big, beautiful world.

It shines brighter now that you are in it.

Dear Baby,

BE

CURIOUS.

Dear Baby,

It's okay to make mistakes.

Get back up and make your mark!

Dear Baby,
There are many ways to say thank you.

Try them all.

Dear Baby,

Put yourself in someone else's shoes.

You'll go far.

Dear Baby,

Explore,

explore,

explore.

There's always more.

Dear Baby,
Remember your roots,
and spread your branches far and wide.

Dear Baby,
You know what's *really* great?
Not taking yourself too

SERIO

OUSLY.

Seriously.

Dear Baby,

Never be afraid to break down walls

and build bridges.

Dear Baby,

Sometimes you will need to
speak up.

Sometimes you will need to
listen.

And sometimes you'll need to do
a little bit of both.

Dear Baby,

Feeling stuck?

Remember, some things in life

take **BABY STEPS.**

Dear Baby,
Wiggle and giggle like no one is watching . . .

even if someone is watching.

Dear Baby,

Look up!

Each star is a spark of possibility.

Dear Baby,

You are exactly

who,

what,

and where

you are supposed to be.

Dear Baby,

I'll always be a helping hand,

but ...

YOU

will paint your own picture.

Dear Baby,

I hope your dreams come true.

Mine did when I met you.

Dear Baby,

You are ready for this

big,

beautiful

world.

And I can't wait to see all that you will do.

Most of all, dear baby who I love,
know that even when we are apart,

I will always,

always,

always